Secret Friends

Elizabeth Laird

MACMILLAN CHILDREN'S BOOKS

First published 1996 by Hodder Children's Books

This edition published 2019 by Macmillan Children's Books
an imprint of Pan Macmillan
The Smithson, 6 Briset Street, London EC1M 9NR
Associated companies throughout the world
www.panmacmillan.com

ISBN 978-1-5290-1540-9

Text copyright © Elizabeth Laird 2019
Illustrations copyright © Alleanna Harris 2019

The right of Elizabeth Laird and Alleanna Harris to be identified as
the author and illustrator of this work has been asserted by them
in accordance with the Copyright, Designs and Patents Act 1988.

1 3 5 7 9 8 6 4 2

A CIP catalogue record for this book is available from
the British Library.

Printed and bound by CPI Group (UK) Ltd, Croydon CR0 4YY

For Hannah

Chapter One

She was the very first person I met on my very first day at Dale Road Secondary School. We bumped into each other at the door of the hall where we'd been sent to wait for our class teachers.

'Oh, sorry,' she said.

'Me too,' I said.

She was much taller than me and quite thin. She had a bush of brown curly hair and pale brown skin which was dotted all over with freckles. But what you noticed straight away was her ears. They were large and stuck out away from her head. Like bats' ears.

'My name's Lucy,' I said.

'I'm Rafaella,' she said.

I don't know what got into me. Perhaps it was the nervousness of starting a new school. Perhaps it was the way she looked down at me, a little aloof, as if I was an interesting insect miles below her.

'I can't call you *that*,' I said bursting into loud laughter. 'I'm going to call you Earwig. Eerie-Eerie-Earwig.'

She flushed up to the roots of her hair and turned away.

I could tell that tears had sprouted behind her eyelids, but she wasn't going to let me see them.

'Sorry,' I said awkwardly. 'Rafaella's a nice name actually. Sort of unusual, but so what?'

It was too late. Other people, standing silently nearby, not yet knowing how to talk to each other, had overheard us.

I saw one boy nudge another and look up at Rafaella's closed pale face.

'Earwig,' he whispered, and they both giggled.

I've often thought I could have stopped it then and there, stood up for

her, got things back on to the right track, but I didn't. I just waited, standing and fiddling with the pleats of my new navy uniform skirt, letting the laughs and the sideways glances go on round the hall.

I'm going to regret that moment till the day I die.

Chapter Two

It's crazy starting at a new school. For days you feel so new and lost it's as if you've wandered into a foreign country where you can't speak the language. Then, all of a sudden, everything falls into place and you feel you've been there for ever.

The people fall into place too. It doesn't

take long to work out who's going to be popular and who's going to be out of it, who's going to get into trouble and who's going to be a teacher's pet.

It was obvious, from that very first day, that Rafaella was going to be an outsider, on the edge of everything, not liked. No one actually hurt her or even teased her much. They just ignored her and left her out of things.

'What do *you* want, Earwig?' a group of girls would say, as Rafaella approached them.

They would stop their conversation to turn and look at her coldly, and she would blush, as she always did, mumble 'Nothing,' and turn away.

I was in those groups sometimes, trying to talk to Kate and Sophie, the two super-popular girls in the class. And I'd watch Rafaella and think, *Not like that, you idiot. Smile. Say something cool. Don't show you care.*

But after school it was different. Rafaella's house was quite near mine and we both had to get off at the same bus stop and walk down the same long road. For the first three weeks of term, we walked one behind the other and neither of us showed by a word or a look that we knew the other was there.

Then, one afternoon, she suddenly ran up behind me and said very quickly, 'Come round to my house for tea.'

And I was so taken by surprise that I said, 'Yes.'

I regretted it at once, of course, and I started talking in a stiff, short way so as not to appear too friendly while she led me down a side road towards a small old house behind a high wooden fence. She didn't seem to notice that I was being so distant. She was as excited as a puppy who's just unearthed a bone.

I felt even more uncomfortable when she opened the front door and I followed her inside.

The house was unlike any I'd been in before. Strange, beautiful pictures hung on the walls and old rugs covered the floors. From the front room I could hear

the sound of sad music and I smelled spicy food.

I wanted to turn and go home at once, but Rafaella said, 'Come in here,' and pushed me into the front room.

Although it was sunny outside, the curtains were half drawn. A red shaded table lamp was on and by its light I saw nothing but books. They were stacked on shelves up to the ceiling, balanced on the old piano, piled up on the floor.

Then I saw the man. He had a white beard and was sitting in the window, a rug over his knees, his glasses slipping down over his nose. He must have been eighty years old at least.

'So,' he said, and I could tell at once that he had a foreign accent. 'Rafaella has brought home a friend.'

He smiled and stretched out a long thin hand, so I had to cross the room and go up to him and shake it though I didn't want to.

'Her name's Lucy, Dad,' said Rafaella.

The old man's hand was surprisingly firm and strong.

'You think I'm too old to be the father

of this little girl?' he said smiling at me and reading my thoughts so accurately that I blushed.

'No, no, of course not,' I stammered, and in fact, now that he was looking up at me, I could see that he had Rafaella's deep set eyes, though his were pale blue, not brown, and that the ears under his bushy white hair were huge.

'Look,' he said, as if he was carrying on a conversation that had been interrupted. 'This picture, so beautiful, so extraordinary, you think so?'

He pointed at the open book on his lap, and I looked down and saw whirling suns and flaming clouds, horsemen trailing banners and tigers leaping.

I wanted to look at it more closely, but Rafaella said, 'She's come for tea, Dad, not for pictures,' and he shut the book obediently.

'Biscuits and buns, better than art, no?' And he winked at me.

I laughed.

He's really nice, I thought, but I couldn't imagine him being a dad. There's no chance my dad would sit looking at a book filled with pictures in the middle of the afternoon, or at any other time of the day come to think of it.

'Darling! Here you are!'

A little woman, dark skinned and with black curly hair, had come into the room. 'How was the torture chamber today?'

She hadn't seen me.

Rafaella pulled me forward.

'This is Lucy, Mum,' she said. 'I've brought her home for tea.'

'How wonderful! How lovely!'

Rafaella's mother seemed really pleased, as if I was a princess or something. She smiled with her whole face, patting my arm with her soft hand.

She looked as young as my mum, but different in every other way. Her clothes were foreign and so was her voice, though not in the same way as her husband's. She might have been from some southern or eastern country. I couldn't tell.

'How lucky,' she said with a chuckle that came from deep in her throat.

'I made sweets today.'

We had tea in the kitchen, sitting round the little table, nibbling at strange things made of honey and nuts. I'd never seen things like that before. I tried one, but I wasn't sure of it and I didn't want any more, so Rafaella fetched out a packet of biscuits and I ate a lot of those.

The three of them kept pouring more tea into my cup and smiling at me and asking me questions as if I was a strange being from outer space, as if I was the first outsider who had ever walked into their house.

'Oh! Your mother!' said Rafaella's mother suddenly. 'She'll be worried so much that you haven't come home!'

'No she won't,' I said. 'She doesn't finish her shift till six.'

I left at last, full of tea and biscuits, feeling good. Rafaella and her mum waved to me as I walked away, standing with their arms round each other's waists.

They really love each other, I thought enviously. *They like being with each other. They're really nice.*

Chapter Three

Kate and Sophie used to hang round the front of the new art block. There's a nice place there, a fence with round metal bars that you can sit on. I used to be there all the time too, laughing when they laughed, listening to everything they said.

The strange thing was that I didn't even like Kate and Sophie much. They were funny, I suppose, always ready for a laugh, but spiteful too. I used to have to watch my back all the time in case the laughter turned on me.

I don't know why I spent so much time trying to get in with them. I didn't later on. I made new friends. Real friends.

We were there one day watching Kate, who was perched on the top bar, doing her impression of Miss Lewis. We were all egging her on.

'Go on, Kate. Do the bit where she falls in love with Mr Warburg.'

'Yeah. When she says, "Oh, Harold..."'

'What?' I couldn't help interrupting.

'Mr Warburg's not really called Harold, is he?'

'Course he is. Everyone knows that. Shut up, Lucy. Go on, Kate.'

'Oh, Ha-Ha-Harold,' Kate started. She put her arms round an imaginary man, closed her eyes and pretended to kiss him, screwing up her lips and making sucking noises. We all doubled over with laughter.

Suddenly I saw Rafaella coming round the corner of the art block towards us. I frowned and looked away. I didn't mind being friends with her out of school. In fact, I'd gone to her house several times. But in school it was different. You were a social outcast if you were seen with

Earwig, and I didn't want to risk it.

Kate was contorting herself into even funnier positions.

'Ooh, Harold!' she was cooing. 'My da-a-arling!'

Rafaella's shoes crunched on the gravel path behind Kate's back.

'Oh, hello, Miss Lewis,' Sophie said loudly, winking at me.

I smiled feebly.

Kate straightened herself up at once and looked round, her face scarlet, her lips visibly struggling to find words of excuse. We all burst out laughing.

'I might have known it,' said Kate glaring furiously at Rafaella. 'Trust you, creeping up on me, pretending to be Miss

Lewis. Buzz off, Earwig.'

'Hey,' I said, shocked at the unfairness of it. 'It was Sophie who . . .'

They both looked at me, then through me, as if I wasn't there.

'You coming?' said Sophie linking her arm through Kate's. 'Let's go round by

the tennis courts. It's not so crowded there.'

I looked at Rafaella. She had said nothing and her face was closed. It looked hard, as if a shell had formed over it.

'See you later,' I said lamely and, feeling treacherous, I followed the others, flicking my hair back over my ears as I had watched Kate doing a hundred times before.

Rafaella ran after me and before I'd caught the others up she darted in front of me, blocking my way.

'Why?' she burst out, and her voice sounded tight as if she was trying not to cry. 'Why do they all hate me so much?'

'They don't hate you,' I said awkwardly. 'It's just . . .'

'Just what? I don't smell, do I? I've never been mean to them. I've never hit any of them, or told on them, or stolen their things . . .'

'They don't hate you,' I said again, 'but you're different at school. Sort of closed up and touchy.'

She wasn't listening.

'It's because of my mum and dad being different,' she said.

'No, I don't think it's that.'

She was worked up, twisting her hands, her voice catching.

'It's my ears, isn't it? It's *these*,' and she put both hands up to her ears and tugged at them as if she was trying to pull them off.

I felt terrible then. I remembered that first day of term and I wanted to tell her how sorry I'd been ever since. But I couldn't find the words.

Tears were rolling down her cheeks now.

'You don't know what it's like,' she said. 'The way they look past me. The way they ignore me. It's like being dead. Like I'm the living dead.'

Chapter Four

I went home with Rafaella after school. That was the day I met her older brother. We had gone up to her bedroom as soon as we got in and had started looking at some clothes.

Rafaella was completely different at home. When she was at school it was as if she had been enclosed in one of those hard cases caterpillars make for themselves, but at home she came out like a butterfly, brilliantly coloured and full of movement. She looked like another person. You only noticed her bright dancing eyes. You never saw those round protruding ears.

She had pulled out of a drawer a piece of the finest, softest white material embroidered in bright colours round the edges.

'What's that?' I asked.

'You're supposed to wrap it round your head,' she said.

'What, me? Are you joking? I'd look daft all tied up like a mummy.'

'No, look. I'll show you.'

She took the thing out of my hands and tied it round my head so that all my hair disappeared. My hair's quite long now and it falls over my forehead and dangles down over my shoulders. But when it had all been tucked away, I looked amazing. I could see the shape of my face in a way I'd never seen it before. It looked completely grown up and even beautiful, like a photograph of a sculpture in one of her dad's books.

'Where did you get it from?' I asked.

'It's my mum's. It's sort of like a national costume. What they wear where she comes from.'

I never asked what that country was. Somehow, I didn't want to know.

Rafaella's parents seemed like magic people to me and their house was an Aladdin's cave, full of treasures whose meaning I couldn't understand.

Rafaella was rifling through a chest of drawers, throwing things out onto her bed. At last she pulled out a thick metal pendant with a dull silver sheen, cut all over in a criss-cross pattern.

'Here, put this on,' she said. 'Then let's go down and show Mum.'

The pendant was on a chain. I clasped it round my neck.

'I feel like a complete idiot,' I said.

Her eyes were dancing with laughter and pleasure.

'No, no, you look brilliant! Mum'll

love it,' and she pushed me towards the door.

I was down the stairs and half way to the kitchen when the front door crashed open. A boy came in.

He was like Rafaella, only taller and even thinner, about eighteen I guessed, with the same pale brown skin and intense dark eyes.

Rafaella's mother came running out of the kitchen.

'Dani, what happened?' she said anxiously. 'Did you get the job?'

'Of course not.'

He didn't look at her. He was looking at me.

'Who's this?' he said, and his voice

wasn't friendly. 'Why's she wearing Mum's things?'

'She's Lucy. She's from my school,' Rafaella said frowning warningly at him.

'From that school? Then you're one of those stuck-up kids who won't go round with my sister! Know what I'd like to do to all of you?'

'Shut up, Dani!' said Rafaella furiously, 'Lucy's my friend!'

'Oh, sorry, I'm sure,' Dani said and as he pushed by me on the way to the kitchen, I felt the heat of his anger as if a fireball had passed by.

'Who is there? What is wrong?' Rafaella's father called out from the sitting room. 'Is it Lucy? Come and see me, Lucy!'

But I was scarlet with embarrassment. I ripped the headdress off, pushed the necklace into Rafaella's hand and groped around for my coat and bag.

'Got to go,' I said. 'Homework,' and ran out of the house.

'Come back, Lucy,' Rafaella called out after me, but I didn't stop.

Anger spurred me down the street and I ran as fast as I could.

What did he want to shout at me like that for? I thought. *I haven't done anything. He's stuck up himself.*

Then I remembered how he had seen me in the headdress and the way his eyes had burned with contempt.

'Suppose he thought I was making fun,'

I muttered, and I burned with shame and embarrassment instead.

I slowed down to a walk and by the time I got home my mixed feelings still weren't sorted out. I was only sure of one thing. I wished I had a brother who'd care as much about what happened to me as Dani cared for Rafaella.

Chapter Five

I went down with flu that weekend and missed a week of school. It was miserable being at home on my own all the time, though my gran came round nearly every day to get me something to eat and keep me company. All I did most of the time was lie on the sofa and watch TV until I was so bored I hated the sight of it.

When I got back to school, still feeling weak in the legs, Rafaella hardly spoke to me. She'd retreated into her hard shell again and gazed down at me with her distant look, like a timid giraffe preparing to bolt from a hungry leopard.

By now it was nearly Christmas time and there were only two weeks to go until the end of term. Miss Lewis had organized a party from the school to sing carols in the town centre one Friday after school.

'Do your bit for charity,' she said to the class brightly and I saw Kate and Sophie exchange speaking looks. They wouldn't have been seen dead in school uniform round a Christmas tree, singing.

I volunteered. I liked doing things after school. It was better than going home to our empty house and Rafaella hadn't invited me back to hers since I'd had flu. I'd had the feeling that she was avoiding me on the way home too. She didn't make a thing about it. She just never seemed to be at the bus stop at the same time as me.

To my astonishment, Rafaella volunteered too. It was the first time she'd done anything out of the ordinary at school. She'd been different all that day, full of suppressed excitement.

'Glad you're coming,' I said a bit shyly, not quite knowing how to break the ice. 'I didn't want to do it without anyone I know.'

She smiled at me and I was surprised and relieved to see that she was wearing her home face, the open, lively, happy one.

'It's going to be fun,' she said, and she twirled around on her dancer's feet.

'What are you looking so pleased about?' I said as we walked together behind Miss Lewis down the hill towards the town centre. I'd probably have walked with her anyway, at least, I hope I would, but it made it much easier that Kate and Sophie weren't around. In fact, Rafaella and I were the only two from our class who had volunteered, so I could relax for once.

She turned to smile at me and I was taken aback by the blaze in her eyes.

'You don't know how pleased I am!' she said, jumping up to touch the branch of a tree that leaned out across the pavement.

'What about?'

'You'll see. You're going to get a surprise after Christmas. A big surprise.'

'What do you mean? What surprise?'

'I can't tell you. It mightn't come out all right. I don't dare tell anyone in case it doesn't happen.'

I went on at her, but she wouldn't say another word. She just shut her mouth and shook her head and beamed at me, her eyes full of laughter.

We stood round the Christmas tree for what seemed like hours, singing 'Away In a Manger' and 'O Come All Ye

Faithful' until our feet were dead with cold and our voices hoarse.

We took turns to rattle the money buckets that people were supposed to put the cash into. The buckets were a bit optimistic, I thought. The money we got would hardly have filled a teacup. But Miss Lewis was pleased.

'Thank you very much, everyone,' she said. 'You've been magnificent.'

She came up to Rafaella and touched her shoulder.

'I hope it all goes very well, dear,' she said.

'What? Why? What's going to go well?' I burst out as soon as Miss Lewis had gone.

Rafaella shook her head.

'You won't make me tell,' she said, 'not even if you torture me.'

She swung her bag off her shoulder and dug down into it.

'Here's your Christmas card,' she said.

I took it.

'Thanks, but it's a bit early, isn't it? We

44

don't break up till the end of the week.'

She pulled her bag back up onto her shoulder.

'I'm not going to be around for the rest of term,' she said. 'This is my last day in school.'

'What? Are you going on holiday, or something?'

'Yes. I'm going away.'

I turned away, offended.

'Thanks for not telling me.'

She shook my arm.

'I couldn't, Lucy. I can't tell anyone. Something's going to happen to me and it's going to change my life. You're the first person I'll tell, the very first, when it's all over. I promise.'

'OK. Suit yourself. See you next term then.'

I wasn't going home straight away. I'd arranged to meet my gran at the café so we could start the search for a Christmas present for Mum. I started walking away.

'Yes, see you!' she called out after me.

'Have a great Christmas. Don't be angry with me!'

I turned then with a brief wave and a smile. She made a tall dark shape against the tinselled, twinkling cone of the huge tree.

I went off to the café feeling let down. It wasn't Rafaella's secret that disturbed me. I realized I was disappointed. I'd been looking forward to seeing her in the Christmas holidays, to going to her house again, feeling its welcoming warmth and glowing light, eating the honey sweets her mum made that I'd really grown to like, listening to her Dad's gentle stories. I wanted very much to see Dani again too, and wipe the contempt out of his eyes.

Chapter Six

I went around feeling angry and rejected for two or three days, telling myself that I didn't miss Rafaella at all. But the truth is that I did, even during school, where I had always found her company embarrassing.

Then, three days before Christmas, I

walked down her street. There was a light on in the sitting room. I recognized the red glow of her father's old lamp, but the other windows were dark and I imagined him sitting in his big chair in the corner by the window, alone in the house, smiling as he turned the pages of one of his books and listening to his lilting music.

It was late in the afternoon but the shops were still open. I had told myself that I wouldn't bother sending Rafaella a Christmas card, but I suddenly wanted to be in touch with her and her family and sending a Christmas card was the only way to do it.

I hurried to the newsagent on the corner of the street. Their selection wasn't brilliant, but I found one I thought she'd like. It was of a Christmas tree, a huge green cone covered in tinsel and twinkling lights with a beautiful golden star at the top.

I bought it, then I saw, on a shelf nearby, a row of funny little fluffy bears, red, yellow and blue. They were tiny, only a few centimeters tall, but they looked so cheeky and pleased with themselves that on an impulse I bought a blue one.

'Mind if I borrow a pen?' I said to the lady behind the counter and she pushed one over to me. I wrote, 'With love from Lucy, have a great Christmas whatever it is you're doing,' put it into the envelope with the little bear, wrote 'Rafaella' on it, and went back out into the dark street.

I felt quite nervous as I ran up to the front door and pushed the card in through the letterbox. I was scared that Dani would come up behind me and look at me that way again.

Quite honestly, I don't remember much about Christmas. Nothing special happened. Mum got into a great state about the cooking, as usual, and Gran came round to help. I had some nice presents, clothes mostly, and we watched some good films.

I kept wondering about Rafaella and her surprise, and about what Christmas would be like in their house. I imagined

it would be exciting, with exotic presents wrapped in richly coloured paper and piles of hot, highly-spiced food, and ceremonies by candlelight. Then I wondered if they'd celebrate Christmas at all. Perhaps they didn't, wherever it was they came from.

The thought made me feel better. Less envious.

Chapter Seven

I was glad when the holidays were over, to be honest. I always am. It's so boring once Mum goes back to work. Even when she's at home we don't seem to know what to say to each other. I'm always pleased to get back into the hearty, crowded rowdiness of school.

'Oh, Gawd, look at me, all those mince pies have given me spots,' said Kate, as she stood in front of the mirror in the cloakroom, inspecting her perfect skin.

'Hey, Soph, let's see your brace,' some others said, crowding round Sophie and laughing as she bared her newly metalled teeth at them.

The bell rang. I looked round for Rafaella but she wasn't there. Disappointed, I followed the others to our classroom.

Miss Lewis took a long time coming and we began to muck about. Some people started drawing faces, and worse, with their fingers in the condensation on the windows. We all fell about laughing.

'She's coming!' someone yelled, and they rubbed out the drawings with their sleeves and scuttled to their seats.

Miss Lewis didn't need to calm us down. One look at her face silenced the class at once. She'd been crying. And behind her was Mr Samson, the head teacher. We looked at them both, agog with curiosity.

Mr Samson cleared his throat.

'Is there a special friend of Rafaella's in this class?' he said.

Nobody moved. I felt my heart begin to beat faster. I was a special friend of Rafaella's, the best she'd got in that class anyway. I was sick of denying it. There and then I made a new resolution. Social death or not, I'd stop pretending. I'd be her friend at school just as much as I was at home.

I stood up. Everyone swivelled round to look at me.

'Go with Mr Samson, dear,' said Miss Lewis. 'He's got something to tell you.'

The walk down the corridor to Mr Samson's office wasn't far but it seemed like miles that day. I couldn't imagine what had happened. Was this Rafaella's surprise? Why was Mr Samson so silent? Something like dread began to grip my heart.

I'd never been into Mr Samson's office before. His secretary watched us as we walked past.

'Bring Lucy a cup of tea,' he said to her.

I couldn't believe this. I was actually sitting in an armchair in Mr Samson's office, stirring sugar into a cup of tea.

Mr Samson leaned forward in his chair towards me.

'Did Rafaella tell you what she was going to do in the holidays?' he said.

'No, sir.'

I felt shy and awkward being in there with him. I could hardly concentrate on what he was saying.

'She only told me I was going to get a big surprise and that she was really excited about something. She wouldn't

tell me anything else.'

'She went into hospital,' Mr Samson said. 'For an operation.'

The dread was growing in my chest, making me feel cold.

'An operation? But she wasn't ill.'

'No. She wasn't ill. It wasn't that kind of operation. It was what they call "corrective surgery".'

I looked at him blankly.

'Perhaps you noticed, Lucy, that Rafaella had rather large ears?'

I nodded.

'I expect she got a bit teased about it now and then, didn't she?' He was speaking very gently.

'Yes. They – we – called her "Earwig".'

'I know.'

He cleared his throat. I realized with surprise that he didn't know how to go on.

'The operation was to pin back and reduce the size of her ears. It's quite a common thing. It would have changed the way she looked. She was desperate to have it done. Quite desperate.'

I waited. I was so cold I was shivering.

'Lucy,' Mr Samson said, 'I'm afraid this will be a dreadful shock to you. Something went wrong when she was under the anaesthetic. She didn't pull through.'

I couldn't take in what he was saying.

'What do you mean, sir? I don't

understand.'

'Rafaella's heart gave way during the operation. There was a defect no one knew anything about. She passed away.'

Everything around me looked strange. The table, the chair, the cup of tea, Mr Samson. *I'm in a dream*, I thought. *I'll wake up in a minute.*

'You mean – she's dead?'

'Yes.'

He sat there looking at me, not knowing what to say, expecting me to burst into tears or to start shouting or something. But I was frozen stiff and the ice inside me had hardened into rock. He was still speaking.

I found it hard to listen.

'If there's anything I can do,' he seemed to be saying, 'if ever you want to come and talk, the door of my office will be open. Don't try to carry this alone, Lucy. Talk to your other friends. Have a good cry. It was a terrible, tragic accident, a one in a million chance. No one's to blame. It was no one's fault, no one's fault at all.'

Chapter Eight

What's worse, guilt or grief? I felt them both, deep down inside, but it was the guilt that really hurt.

Mr Samson said I could go home for the rest of the day. It seemed like a good idea. I didn't want to face the others. I went to Gran's house but she was out, so I spent the rest of the morning wandering around town on my own.

The Christmas tree had gone, of course, with all the rest of the tinselly stuff, and the sales were on.

The place was busy. I stood near where I'd last seen Rafaella, in the shopping mall where we'd sung carols together, and I tried to remember her face. The funny thing was that I couldn't see it clearly. I could only see her outline, as it had been against the tree. It seemed incredible, impossible, that she had gone forever.

Suddenly, in the distance, I saw a girl in a navy coat walking away from me round a corner.

It's her! I thought with a shock of

relief. *Mr Samson's got it wrong. He made a mistake.*

I darted after the girl, pushing past irritated shoppers, and when I came round the corner I nearly bumped into her. She was standing still, looking into a shop window. She wasn't Rafaella. She didn't even look like her.

I sat down on a bench and my chest began to heave.

'I'm sorry, I'm sorry, I'm sorry,' I kept saying under my breath. 'Sorry for not standing up for you. Sorry for not being your friend at school. Sorry for calling you Earwig.'

It was hot in the shopping mall. I knew my face was bright red, from the heat and

the tears. People were looking at me.

'What's that child doing out of school?' I heard a woman say.

I'll have to face them sometime, I thought. Might as well get it over with, so, slowly, I walked back towards the school.

It was lunch break. Everyone was out in the playground. They stood around in little knots talking quietly.

I saw Kate and Sophie at once. They were red-eyed.

Hypocrites, I thought. *Murderers*.

I was going to walk past them, but Kate said, 'Oh, Lucy, isn't it awful?' and she looked so upset that I stopped.

'We had no idea,' Sophie said, 'that she was going to have an operation. Why didn't she say?'

'It would have been great if she'd had her ears fixed,' said Kate. 'She might have turned out really pretty.'

'You must be feeling awful,' said Sophie, squeezing my arm. 'We didn't know poor old Earwig was such a good friend of yours.'

I shook her hand off.

'Don't!' I shouted. 'Don't *ever* call her that again! Her name was Rafaella, right? Rafaella!'

Sophie was offended.

'OK,' she said. 'No need to go crazy on me. You started it. You called her Earwig on the first day of term, remember?'

I was crying again.

'Of course I remember! Don't you understand? It was why she died. She couldn't bear her ears. She felt awful about them. She thought that was why no one liked her. She thought that if she had them fixed she'd be popular. I know it was me that started everyone calling her Earwig. I feel like a murderer.'

There was silence.

Then Kate said quietly, 'It wasn't you, Lu. It was the rest of us. We were much worse than you. And it wasn't just calling her Earwig either. We were awful to her. We're all murderers.'

Sophie had been kicking at a pile of

gravel with the toe of her shoe. Now she said angrily, 'That's daft. You heard what Miss Lewis said. Ear– I mean, Rafaella had a heart defect. She'd have died anyway if she'd had her tonsils out, or got flu or something. We never killed her.'

'Yeah,' said Kate, 'you're right. We didn't really, but I wish we'd been nicer to her, all the same.'

Chapter Nine

It was amazing how quickly the gap that Rafaella left at school closed over. For a few days everyone was rather solemn and unusually nice to me, then they forgot, and two weeks later it was as if Rafaella had never even been at the school. I needn't have worried that people would go on calling her Earwig. They never spoke about her at all.

But the gap didn't close over inside me. It grew deeper and wider. It bled. I would come home to our cold dark house and wish and wish that I was still a welcome guest in her warm bright one.

After a while school wasn't too bad. I made a few new friends and I didn't feel the need to follow the crowd any more. But at night I had to drive the image of Rafaella out of my mind before I could get to sleep. I only ever thought of her as sad and angry. I never remembered the good times we had had.

One night I dreamed about her so vividly that I remember the dream still.

She was at home with her family, happy and lively, but the room slowly changed. The red shaded lamp disappeared, the books and pictures and rugs faded away and we were all at a cold dingy railway station.

'I've got to go away,' Rafaella said as she climbed into a dark train.

'And it's your fault, your fault,' her mum and dad and Dani all said together, pointing their fingers accusingly at me.

When I woke up my pillow was wet with tears. The dream was so real that I couldn't shake it off. I had a desperate desire to see the three of them, to tell them I was sorry, that I had truly wanted to be Rafaella's friend.

My parents were asleep, but that wasn't surprising. They always slept late on a Saturday morning. I scrambled into my clothes, left a note for them and ran down the road to the familiar little house behind the high wooden fence, anxious to get there before I lost my courage.

Chapter Ten

There was a long silence after I'd pressed the doorbell.

They've gone away, I thought, and a dreadful, cold desolation wrapped itself round me.

Then the door suddenly opened.

I'd expected to see Rafaella's dad,

leaning on his stick, or her mum, wiping her hands on a towel, but it was Dani who stood there. He was still in his pyjamas and his hair was rumpled as if he'd only just woken up.

'Hello,' he said. 'What are you doing here? It's only half past seven.'

I hadn't looked at the time. I hadn't known it was so early.

'Sorry,' I said. 'I didn't realize. Sorry to bother you. It wasn't that important anyway.'

He shot out a long arm and pulled me in through the front door.

'You're freezing,' he said. 'Why didn't you put on a coat? Here, take this.'

He reached out for a jacket that hung

on a peg behind the door and threw it round my shoulders.

'I shouldn't have come,' I said, 'but I had a terrible dream and I wanted to see your mum and dad and tell them I was sorry.'

'Lucy!'

I looked up. Rafaella's parents were standing at the top of the stairs in their dressing gowns. They seemed to have grown smaller, as if they had shrunk in on themselves.

Rafaella's mum came down the stairs slowly, as if all her joints were stiff. She didn't say anything, but stood shaking her head as though she had just heard some news that she could not believe.

She held a tissue to her lips and her eyes were fixed on me as if she was seeing me for the first time.

'The child is shivering,' Rafaella's father said. 'Come into the warm. Dani, put on the gas fire.'

We went into the sitting room.

'I dreamed about her, about Rafaella, and about all of you last night,' I said. 'You were angry with me. I know it was all my fault. I started it all, but I didn't mean to . . . I never knew she'd . . . She didn't even tell me about the operation.'

Rafaella's mum began to say something but her voice was choked up with tears. Her husband put out his hand to stop her speaking.

'Wait, my dear,' he said. 'Let her say what she has come to say.' He settled himself painfully in his chair. 'What was your fault, Lucy?'

'On the first day of term, the day I first met Rafaella. I laughed at her name. I said I'd call her Earwig instead. The others heard me. They always called her Earwig after that. They were horrid to her. They used to look at her as if she wasn't there. She said – she said it was like being one of the living dead.'

I sat down on the floor, put my face in my hands and sobbed like I hadn't done before. Then I smelt a soft powdery smell as Rafaella's mum bent down and pushed a tissue into my hand. I felt something else too. An arm, thin but very strong, went round my shoulders and shook me gently.

'You know what,' Dani said. 'You're talking a load of rubbish.'

I was so surprised I stopped crying and looked at him. 'Rafaella said you were the only good thing about that school, the only person who kept her going. She nearly killed me when I was so horrible to you that time you came here.'

'But I was the one who called her Earwig!'

'It was better than what they called her at her last school. She was "Batty" there.'

'But I went off with all the others! I left her on her own!'

'She understood. "Lucy and me are secret friends", she used to say. "She's not like the others. She makes school bearable." That's what she said.'

I looked over his head into his mother's eyes. There was no anger there, only grief, a grief that seemed almost to drown her.

'Lucy,' his dad said. 'Dani is right. You were a real friend to Rafaella. Listen, why don't you go up to her room and take something of hers that you can keep. You would like that, wouldn't you?'

I nodded and jumped up.

I knew that if I looked at Rafaella's mum again the tears would fall faster than ever.

I was glad that none of them came

upstairs with me. I wanted to be on my own.

I pushed open the door of Rafaella's bedroom and went in.

It was just as it had been before. Her bed was made up. Her school skirt hung from a hanger behind the door and her school books were stacked on the table. Propped up on them in pride of place was the Christmas card I'd sent her.

I looked round helplessly. It seemed wrong to open her drawers and look through them. Instead I let my eye wander along a shelf where she had kept some books and a few little ornaments.

A small parcel wrapped in Christmas paper caught my eye. I lifted it down. It

was labelled 'Lucy'. I tore the paper off.
Inside was a little yellow bear, a twin of
the blue one I'd given her. There was a
note too.

It said:

Dear Lucy,

Thanks a million for my little
bear. He's brilliant. I'm going to take
him into hospital with me to keep me
company. Isn't it funny, I'd already
bought this one for you but I forgot
to put it in with my card. I wanted
to give you a bigger present because
you're a brilliant friend but I couldn't
find anything I liked better. Have a
lovely Christmas. See you next term.
You won't recognize me!!!

Love,

Rafaella

I stood there for a long time. Then I heard someone at the door. I turned round. It was Rafaella's mum.

I couldn't say a word. I just held out the letter and the little yellow bear. She took them, and read the letter silently.

'Oh, Lucy,' she said. 'I am so sorry. She gave these to me to post to you but I forgot all about them. So the little blue bear was a present from you? I never guessed. We found it after . . .'

I burst out crying again then. I couldn't help it. And she did too. And we put our arms round each other and cried and cried. We stopped at last and dried our eyes.

'I don't think I can take anything else

of hers,' I said. 'It doesn't seem right, somehow.'

'We'll think about it another time,' she said. 'It's so cold up here. Come down to the kitchen. I'll make you some breakfast.'

'I couldn't eat a thing,' I said.

She smiled sadly.

'Neither could I.'

'Are you two coming downstairs?' Dani called up. 'I've got the breakfast ready.'

Rafaella's mum and I looked at each other and laughed shakily.

'Lucy,' she said. 'Dear Lucy. You'll come back often to visit us, won't you? I couldn't bear to lose you too.'

I followed her out of the room and gently closed the door behind me. Then I followed her downstairs to the warmth and light of her kitchen.

Turn the page to read the opening chapters
of Elizabeth Laird's award-winning first
novel, *Red Sky in the Morning*

Highly Commended for the CILIP Carnegie Medal

*Red Sky
in the
Morning*

From the prize-winning author
Elizabeth Laird

Chapter One

As long as I live, I shall never forget the night my brother was born. For one thing, I didn't get a wink of sleep. I'd only been in bed a few minutes when I heard Dad talking on the telephone. My bedroom's pretty small, and if I lean out of bed far enough I can open the door without actually getting out of bed, so I did, and I heard Dad say,

'That's right, the second house on the left past the shops. And please hurry.'

His voice sounded so urgent I guessed at once he must be calling the ambulance and I knew my time had come. Well, it was Mum's time really, but mine too, in a way, because I was going to be in charge while she was away. I'd practised everything in my mind, so I just got calmly out of bed, and put on my dressing gown, and groped around for my glasses. Then I went calmly out of the room and walked down the hall to Mum and Dad's bedroom. I didn't even run.

'Now just relax, Mum,' I said. 'Everything's under control.' I must have said it too calmly because no one took any notice. Mum's face was screwed up, and Dad was looking at her, standing quite still, with one leg in his trousers and the other out. He looked perfectly ridiculous. Then Mum's face went ordinary again, and she turned her head and saw me, and she looked quite normal. In fact, she gave me a smile. Then Dad started pulling on his trousers again. It was like starting up a video again after a freeze frame.

After that, everything I'd planned to say was swept out of my head, because things happened too fast. Mum's face screwed up again, and she started taking loud, rasping breaths. I've never seen such an awful look in anyone's eyes, not even in a war film.

Dad grabbed his jacket, and pushed past me out of the room. Then I suppose he must have realized it was me, because he came back and ruffled my hair the way he does when he wants to be nice to me. I hate it, but I don't like hurting his feelings, so I just suffer in silence.

'Be a nice girl,' he said. 'Go and get me a cup of tea. The ambulance won't be here for another five minutes. I've got to go and phone your granny.'

I couldn't believe it. I've never heard anything so callous in all my life. There was his wife, probably dying, in the most awful agony, trying to give birth to his own child, and all he could think of were his own selfish pleasures. I realized how woman has suffered from man's selfishness since time began.

'Sorry, Dad,' I said with dignity. 'I expect Mum needs me. You'll find the tea in the usual place.'

But then Mum gave an awful scream, and Dad rushed back into the bedroom and shut the door in my face. I didn't dare go in. I didn't even want to any more. I felt too small and helpless. Frightful thoughts rushed through my mind, like what would happen if Mum died, and I had to sacrifice my youth to looking after Dad and bringing up Katy, who was seven, and absolutely horrible.

The minute I thought of Katy, I remembered my responsibilities. It was my job to run the house and family while Mum was otherwise engaged, and I decided I had better start by running Katy. I went back down the corridor to her room.

Katy is an unusually irritating child. Even Mum admits that she's a nuisance. She says it's because Katy's going through a stage, but either Mum's wrong, or else it's a very long stage, because Katy seems to have been in it since she was born. One of the worst things about her is that you can never get her to go to sleep. We all have to creep around the house once she's gone to bed, and I can't even play my own tapes in my own room, which I feel, quite frankly, is a violation of my human rights. And she wakes up in the middle of the night if a moth so much as brushes its wings against her bedroom window. I never would have thought she'd sleep through the noise Mum was making, but that's the maddening thing about Katy. She's so unpredictable. There wasn't a sound coming from her room. I knelt down, and looked through the keyhole. She always has a nightlight on because she thinks she's so delicious that witches are just dying to come and eat her in the night, so I could see clearly enough that she was fast asleep.

'Well,' I thought, 'that gives me one less thing to worry about,' but at the same time I almost wished Katy had been awake, because I hadn't got anything to do. I certainly wasn't intending to betray Mum by making Dad a cup of tea.

Then I realized that I could at least phone Granny, which Dad seemed to have forgotten about, so I went downstairs to the phone in the hall, and was just beginning to dial when the front doorbell went. The ambulance had come.

There were only two ambulancemen but they filled up our small downstairs hall completely. It's so narrow that if two people meet, one of them has to turn sideways and stand against the wall while the other squashes past. I used to think of ways of making sure it wasn't me who had to stand against the wall, like pretending, if I was holding something, that it was very heavy, or being in a hurry for the loo, but I stopped all that kind of childish thing years ago. Still, I've never stopped minding that our hall is so mean and small, not like Debbie's (she used to be my best friend), and suddenly I got worried about it.

How would they get Mum down the stairs on a stretcher? Supposing it stuck, like that time when Dad was fitting units in their bedroom, and he and Mum were trying to get the old wardrobe down the stairs? It got completely wedged between the wall and the banisters, and Dad had to get a saw and cut it in half before it took off any more wallpaper. He was furious, and it took hours to free the wardrobe. But Mum hadn't got hours. If she got stuck on her stretcher, she'd have to have the baby right there on the stairs.

As it happened, Mum didn't need a stretcher at all. Dad came out of the bedroom, looking pale and shaky and awful, and the men ran upstairs, and then one rushed out again and said,

'Where's the telephone, love?'

And he dialled, and when I heard him talking I started to feel trembly myself, and sick.

'This is Alan here,' he said. 'I've got an emergency over on Blythe Road. Lady in labour. Too far gone to get her to hospital. She's started pushing, and the baby's almost there. Stan's doing what he can, but he says it's not looking quite right. Best get a doctor over here quick. We've got the oxygen and stuff, but we haven't got all the neo-natal kit if they need to do full resuscitation.'

He must have forgotten about me, because he started off up the stairs again when he'd put the receiver down. I couldn't bear to let him go. I had to know what was going on.

'Is – is everything all right?' I said. It sounded more feeble than it meant to, but I didn't know what to say. I was frightened.

'Course it is,' he said. He was using that awful cheerful voice they use to children when they want to deceive them. 'Just a precaution. Your mummy's going to be fine. So's the baby, I expect. It all happened just a bit too quick, that's all.'

He patted my shoulder just as if he'd been a relative. I was only twelve then, but I was mature for my age, and it was not surprising that I felt offended.

'I'm quite prepared to give blood, if necessary,' I said. The idea made me feel sick, but if Mum needed my blood, there was naturally no more to be said. He had the cheek to laugh.

'Oh, we won't need your blood,' he said. 'Best thing you can do is be a good girl and keep out of the way. Tell you what, do you know how to make a cup? Why don't you put the kettle on, then? Me and Stan could do with a cuppa when we've finished with this lot.'

If he hadn't put it like that, of course, I wouldn't have dreamed of making a cup of tea. But I knew that if I didn't he'd think I didn't know how to, so I went to the kitchen, and filled up the kettle. But all the time it was boiling, and while I was putting mugs and milk and sugar on to the tray, I kept thinking about Mum and the baby.

Up until then, I hadn't thought about the baby much as a real person. Quite honestly, I'd been shocked when Mum told me she was pregnant. I couldn't imagine her and Dad having sex. The whole idea seemed disgusting. Especially in our house. Their bedroom didn't look right for it. It was too ordinary. But I'd got used to her getting bigger, and being tired, and relying on me more for things. In some ways I'd enjoyed it. I got quite good at doing a fry-up for supper, and heating up pizzas in the oven. I could even do lamb chops and two veg, though it took hours to peel the potatoes.

Somehow, though, I hadn't thought much about the baby. I'd wanted a brother, I knew that much, mainly because I didn't want another Katy round the place, and I'd started knitting a cardigan, but I'm not much good at knitting, so I'd pulled it undone and tried to learn to crochet instead. But it got in a tangle, so I never managed to get anything finished. Dad had got the pram down out of the attic, and Mum had lined the cot again in some new flowery material. It looked pretty, waiting there all clean and empty, beside her bed, but I hadn't been able to imagine a real, live baby in it.

Then I remembered something I'd read about in a Victorian novel. Grandma's got a whole stack of them, that she used to read about a hundred and fifty years ago. They have titles like *Lost in London*, and

Little Faith, and they're all horribly sad and religious. The children go around bare foot in the snow, selling matches, and their mothers are gin-sodden, and the babies die, and when you read them you cry and cry. I even got sinusitis once, because I cried so much over *Christie's Old Organ*. But I like them too. After I've read one, I feel pure, and refined, and ready to face death.

Anyway, when babies are born in those old books, the mother's poor eldest daughter is always sent to the kitchens to boil gallons of water. It never explained what the water was for, but I knew that was the right thing to do. So I got out the pressure cooker, and the biggest pans I could find, and filled them up, and turned on every burner on the stove. I slopped a bit on the floor, but I managed all right.

It took quite a long time, finding everything, and filling them up, and I was still at work when Dr Randall came. He went up the stairs two at a time, and then another ambulance came, and the men took this funny box thing upstairs. After a while they came down again, holding it carefully, and drove away. The doctor was still there. I could hear him in Mum and Dad's bedroom, which is right above the kitchen. But the rest of the house was quiet. Then I realized that the first ambulancemen, Alan and Stan, had gone too, and they hadn't even bothered to have their cup of tea. I knew then for certain that they'd just been humouring me, and trying to keep me out of the way. Typical!

It was so quiet upstairs that I began to feel a bit worried. What could they all be doing? Was Mum all right? And shouldn't the baby be crying? Mum had promised that I'd be the first after Dad to see it, but no one had called me. I wanted desperately to know what was going on. But I felt too scared to go up and open the bedroom door and just walk in. Medical things seem kind of holy to me. Bursting in on the doctor doing something would be as bad as jumping up in church and shouting 'Hi there!' to the vicar.

Then I remembered the tea. Surely everyone would really and truly want a cup of tea by this time. After all, it was practically morning. The kitchen window was filling with a sort of greyish light, and there were red streaks across the sky. I'd never seen the dawn before. It was eerie and grand. Suitable for a birth, really. I checked that I'd put out enough mugs, filled the teapot (the kettle had boiled ages ago) and staggered upstairs with the tray. Then I put it down, and opened the door a crack, and picked it up, and went in, holding the tray in front of me so it would be the first thing they all saw.

I could see at once that they'd been having a very deep conversation. Mum was lying back in bed, looking white and tired, and Dad was sitting beside her, holding one of her hands. Dr Randall was on the other side of the bed, looking serious. Mum saw me first.

'Oh Annie!' she said, and gave a wobbly kind of laugh, and then Dad jumped up and came towards me, and made a big fuss about taking the tray. I wasn't fooled. I knew he was trying to stop me seeing Mum cry. I knew quite well that that was what she was doing.

'Where is it? Is it a boy? Can't I see him yet?' I whispered to Dad. He just stood there, not saying anything. Then he turned, with the tray in his hands, and looked over to Dr Randall, and Dr Randall came towards me and said in that stupid voice they never use to each other,

'Yes, Anna, you've got a dear little brother, but he's not very well, and we've had to take him to hospital.'

'That box,' I whispered. Somehow I couldn't

bring myself to speak normally. 'He was in that box, wasn't he? Is he . . .?'

Dr Randall smiled for the first time.

'No, he's not dead, Anna. That was only an incubator. It's a special box for babies that need extra warmth and attention. He's not going to die. But . . .'

Now it was his turn to stop and look at Dad, and this time Dad was great. He just put his hands on my shoulders.

'Your brother's not quite right,' he said. 'Dr Randall thinks he may be disabled. We won't be able to tell yet, for a week or two, but it doesn't look . . .' and then the worst possible thing happened. Dad actually cried. He didn't sob or anything. He just crumpled up a bit. That set me off, of course. I've never been able not to cry if someone else is. It's infectious, like giggling, or yawning or something. And then Mum started, and we were all crying, and I felt really sad, but one horrible part of me was looking on from outside, and thinking,

'Well, well. Fancy Mum and Dad and me all crying together over a serious family matter, and Katy still being asleep. That makes me feel really one of them.'

I still couldn't imagine the baby. I knew with my brain that it was sad, him being disabled, but I couldn't really feel it, if you know what I mean.

It's funny how you feel when you stop crying, if you've been crying with someone else. It's embarrassing of course, but quite comfortable too, in a way. You feel loving, and close together, and empty, too.

After a bit, I began to think awful thoughts. What did disabled mean? Would he look funny? Would his legs and arms jerk a lot? Somehow, because we'd all been crying together, I felt especially daring, so I came right out with it to Dr Randall.

'What do you mean, disabled?' I said.

Dr Randall shook his head.

'I was just telling your parents, Anna,' he said. 'We don't know yet. We'll have to wait and see.'

'Yes, but will he be blind, or deaf?' I asked.

Mum and Dad were sitting in a specially still kind of way, and I knew they were dying for the answer too. Dr Randall looked more cheerful.

'Oh no, I'm sure he'll be able to see and hear all right,' he said.

'Will he look nice, or will he look funny, and dribble and all that?' I asked. It sounds awful, but I cared about that more than anything.

'I don't know, Anna,' Dr Randall said. 'I honestly don't know. But all babies are very sweet, you know, even when they're . . .' he stopped.

'Can't you even tell us,' I said, 'if he'll be able to play, and go to school, and talk, and laugh, and everything?'

The cheerful look wiped itself off Dr Randall's face.

'He'll be able to laugh,' he said slowly. 'Oh yes, I'm sure he'll laugh. But for the rest, let's wait and see, shall we? I think we all need some sleep now.' He patted Mum's hand.

'You should try to rest,' he said. 'I'm sure you're very tired. You've done well to manage a home delivery with a birth of this kind. Quite unusual, in fact. I've given you a good strong dose. Make the most of it. You can phone the hospital any time, but there won't be any news until tomorrow morning. The nurse will be here to sort you out at breakfast time. And try not to worry. He's quite stable, you know. There's no danger.'

He picked up his bag and clicked it shut. He seemed suddenly in a hurry to go. The strain, I suppose. Mum always says that emotional upsets are

more exhausting than anything else. Still, he didn't
have much to upset him. It wasn't *his* baby that
wasn't going to run about. All in the day's work for
him, I should think.

He'd only been gone half a minute when he poked
his head round the door again.

'There seems to be rather a lot of steam coming
out of the kitchen,' he said.

Steam! Boiling water! Of course! I'd left the four
burners on full blast. I jumped up like a startled
rabbit, and squeezed past Dr Randall and was in
the kitchen in a flash. There was so much steam I
could hardly see the cooker. Fortunately, none of
the saucepans had boiled dry, but the walls were
streaming with water. I felt such a fool. I was afraid
they'd laugh at me. Dr Randall had never even
mentioned needing any boiling water. I decided I'd
try to empty all the saucepans, and clear up quickly
before Dad came down and saw, and then I could say
that in my excitement I'd left the kettle on. But it
was too late. Dad came into the kitchen right behind
me.

'Very sensible, Spanner,' he said, in a matter of
fact voice. He's always calling me silly names that
rhyme with 'Anna'. It drives me crazy sometimes,

especially if he forgets and does it in front of other people. It sounds so weird. But he won't stop. He just laughs, and says, 'You know what they say, "A loved child has many names," so you be grateful, Gloriana.'

I was relieved, anyway, that he didn't laugh.

'Well,' I said, 'I know boiling water is the right thing to do when a baby's born, but quite honestly, I don't know what it's for.'

Dad didn't seem very sure either.

'Oh, sterilizing instruments or something, I suppose,' he said vaguely. 'Anyway, we'd better go to bed now. There's not much of tonight left.'

But I didn't feel tired at all. Not yet, anyway. I knew I'd feel awful the next day. But just now there were too many things I wanted to know.

'Does it always hurt that bad?' I blurted out. I hadn't meant to ask Dad that, but I couldn't help myself.

'Does what hurt?' he said. I excused him for being so thick and insensitive on the grounds that he was an ignorant male and didn't know any better.

'Having a baby, of course,' I said. 'Mum's face, and then the way she screamed . . .'

'You'll have to ask her,' he said. 'I wouldn't

know, would I? But Mum seems to think it's worth it. It's how you and Kate were born, after all.'

'And now you've got a son, too,' I said, and then I wished I hadn't said it, because Dad looked very sad.

'Yes,' he said. 'And now I've got a son. Come on Susanna. It's bedtime.'

ABOUT THE AUTHOR

Elizabeth Laird is the author of dozens of much-loved children's books, including *The Garbage King*, *The Fastest Boy in the World*, *Oranges in No Man's Land* and the UKLA award-winning *Welcome to Nowhere*. She has been shortlisted for the prestigious CILIP Carnegie Medal six times.

Elizabeth has lived in different countries in the Middle East and Africa and now lives in Britain, but she still likes to travel as much as she can.

ABOUT THE ILLUSTRATOR

Alleanna Harris is a US illustrator who has
been drawing for as long as she can remember.
Alleanna finds inspiration in the beauty of
everyday things. She lives in New Jersey.

'Sings with truth' The Times

Forced to flee his home in Syria, Omar and his family face the dangers of civil war. A moving story of conflict and hope, winner of the UKLA Book Award.

A powerful story about the importance of ocean conservation and looking after your environment from the award-winning author, Elizabeth Laird.